Written by Elizabeth Wood

Illustrated by Neal Yamamoto

Manufactured in the United States of America.

ISBN: 0-929923-93-6
Library of Congress Cataloging-in-Publication Card No.: 92-7814

10 9 8 7 6 5

Lowell House House
Juvenile
Los Angeles
CONTEMPORARY
BOOKS
Chicago

Quick Freeze

You can magically turn water into ice without a freezer!

What You'll Need

- sponge
- paper cup
- glue
- scissors
- water
- pitcher
- ice cube

Getting Ready

Cut the sponge to fit snugly into the bottom of the cup. Secure it with a little glue. Right before you perform this trick, secretly place the ice cube at the bottom of the cup.

Show Time!

1. Pour a *little* water from the pitcher into the cup and say, "This ordinary water will now magically disappear."
2. Now ask a volunteer from the audience to kindly join you on the stage.
3. Slowly pour the ice cube from the cup into the volunteer's hand.
4. Say, "I really tried to make the water *disappear*, but it was just too *hard*!"

When you pour the water into the cup, the sponge soaks it all up!

SECRETLY PLACE ICE IN CUP

SECRETLY GLUE SPONGE TO BOTTOM

NOTE: The three cards in the upper right-hand corner indicate the level of difficulty of each magic trick, 1 being the easiest and 3 the hardest.

Big Squeeze

Squeeze a little glass of water so tightly that it vanishes into thin air!

What You'll Need

- a black elastic cord that is a little shorter than your arm
- a staple or pin
- safety pin
- a hard rubber ball that will fit tightly into the mouth of the glass
- small shot glass

Getting Ready

Attach one end of the cord to the ball with the staple or pin. Tie the other end of the cord to the safety pin. Fasten the safety pin with the cord tied to it to the inner lining of your magician's jacket at the top of the right shoulder (A). The cord and rubber ball should hang three inches *above* the bottom of your jacket. If the cord is too long, cut it from the top and retie it to the safety pin.

Show Time!

1. While standing in front of the audience, pretend you have an itch. The itch should be near your right hip. Reach into your jacket with your right hand and pretend to scratch. Take the hanging ball into your hand as you do this. As you withdraw your hand, make sure your knuckles are facing the audience and that the ball is well concealed in your palm with your last three fingers holding the ball in place. This technique is known as *palming,* and although it may feel funny, it is a very effective way to hide small objects. And, if you relax your other fingers, it makes you look like a great showman.

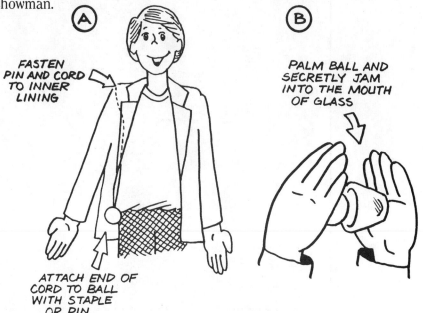

Ⓐ FASTEN PIN AND CORD TO INNER LINING

ATTACH END OF CORD TO BALL WITH STAPLE OR PIN

Ⓑ PALM BALL AND SECRETLY JAM INTO THE MOUTH OF GLASS

2. Pick up the glass with your left hand and point to it with your right hand (with ball still concealed). Say, "I've been practicing my powers of strength, and yesterday I squeezed a glass like this into thin air. Let's see if I can do it again."

3. Put your right hand on top of the glass and squeeze the glass between both hands with all your might. While you are squeezing, jam the secret ball into the mouth of the glass until it is tightly stuck (B), and straighten your arms out and down to stretch the elastic cord.

4. Turn slowly to your left and then suddenly throw your hands up into the air and yell "Shazam!" The glass will be pulled into your jacket so quickly that no one will see it disappear. Your hands will be empty!

NOTE: This trick requires lots of practice. When it is performed well, you will earn everyone's respect.

Classic Cups And Balls

Learn a classic cups-and-balls trick like the one magicians perform around the world, swiftly passing cups through balls and balls through cups. You'll be amazed to learn how easy this trick really is!

What You'll Need

• 3 cups   • 4 balls, either sponge or paper

(The cups must be stackable so that they "nest" together. They must also be tapered so the balls fit between the cups when they are stacked, without being noticed. The cups must be of a solid material so no one can see through them.)

Getting Ready

Place a ball into one of the cups. Stack, or nest, the three cups, *mouths up*, on a table. The cup containing the ball goes in the middle of the stack (A). Place the remaining three balls in the top cup.

Show Time!

1. Pick up the cups together in one stack and spill the three balls onto the table. This lets everyone see the balls.

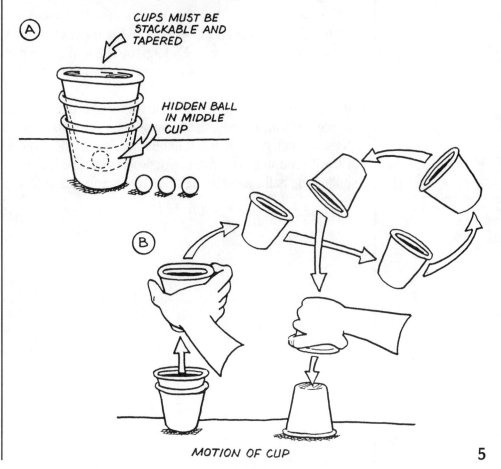

(A) CUPS MUST BE STACKABLE AND TAPERED

HIDDEN BALL IN MIDDLE CUP

(B)

MOTION OF CUP

2. THE HARD PART: Everyone should see each empty cup but not the secret ball. Holding the stack of cups upright, take the top cup with your free hand and swoop the cup up and down through the air, then set it mouth down on the table (B). Repeat with the middle cup (the secret-ball cup). Place it over the upside-down cup on the table. (You should practice this several times beforehand so the ball doesn't roll out.) Place the third cup, in the same manner, upside down on the other two.

NOTE: Swooping your hand through the air actually helps force the ball to stay in the cup when it is upside down for a short time.

3. Tell the audience that you have no tricks up your sleeve. Pick up the cups in the stack, turning them right side up. One at a time, place them *mouths down* on the table, side by side. The cup with the secret ball in it will be in the middle. Remember to swoop each cup through the air before you put them on the table!

4. Pick up one of the three balls that you spilled out in Step 1 and place it on top of the middle cup. Cover it with the other cups, tap your wand on top and say, "Hocus Pocus!" Pick up the stack with one hand. Presto! The ball on the table must have gone right through the cup!

NOTE: This trick requires lots and lots of practice in order to achieve a flawless performance. The great thing about it is that once you've memorized the steps, you can perform it just about anywhere! Once you've become comfortable with the steps and can easily swoop and turn the cups over without spilling the balls, you can make up your own routine.

4 Five Glass Jive

Five glasses are lined up full, empty, full, empty, full. Ask a volunteer to change the order to three full glasses on the right, two empty glasses on the left—in one swift move, with one hand! Only you have the know-how to do it.

What You'll Need

• 5 glasses
• water

Getting Ready

Fill three of the five glasses with water. Line them up on a table in the following manner: full, empty, full, empty, full.

Show Time!

1. After several people try to change the order of the glasses, simply take the full glass on the right end and pour the water into the empty glass second from the left.

NOTE: Your friends will probably want to throw the water on *you* after this trick, so you'd better run!

Tip Over Tube

With your magic tube, change a white ball to red and back to white again!

What You'll Need

For the Tip Over Tube:
- 2 small, empty vegetable cans (3¼ inches high, 2½ inches wide)
- colored adhesive tape
- black contact paper
- scissors

For the trick:
- the finished Tip Over Tube
- 2 rubber balls: one red, one white

Getting Ready

To make the Tip Over Tube, place cans bottom-to-bottom. Wrap tape around the middle so they stay together. Wrap black contact paper around the whole tube to completely cover the cans. Decorate the tube with colorful tape and glitter any way you like.

Show Time!

1. Stand the tube on one end and hide the red ball in the top part. Place the white ball next to the tube.
2. In front of the audience, pick up the tube slowly from the bottom. Quickly turn it over and put it down so the red ball does not fall out. Practice this several times. You'll be surprised how easy this is to do.
3. Drop the white ball into the top compartment of the tube. Your audience will expect the white ball to fall through, but when you pick up the tube, the ball underneath will be red!
4. To change the red ball back to white, turn the tube over again in the same, swift way, and drop the red ball into the top of the tube.
5. Lift the tube again and show that the red ball has turned back to white!

TWO CANS ARE TAPED TOGETHER BOTTOM-TO-BOTTOM

SECRETLY PLACE RED BALL IN THE TOP TUBE

What Water?

This marvelous trick is perfect for a real wiseguy. It is also very easy. The magician makes water disappear with a flick of a light switch.

What You'll Need

- drinking straw
- glass ¾ full of water
- colored or white adhesive tape

Getting Ready

Before performing this trick, practice drinking very quietly through the straw. Then hide the straw in your pocket.

Show Time!

1. Tape the glass of water to the table. Explain to your audience that you are going to make the water in the glass disappear without moving the glass or the tape. (Fastening the glass down is a little Houdini-like and will add some drama and suspense.)

2. Close your eyes and appear to be concentrating *very* hard. Pretend that you are trying to make the water go away with the power of your mind. Take a peek at your progress by opening one eye. When you see that nothing has happened, act really embarrassed. Ask for total darkness because you can't stand the embarrassment.

3. When your assistant turns out the lights, stomp up and down, bang your fists, and make a lot of noise. In the meantime, take out the straw. Use the noise as a distraction while you quickly and silently drink the water through the straw. Leave a little water at the bottom of the glass so you don't slurp and give the trick away. Quickly pop the straw back into your pocket.

4. Have your assistant flick the light back on while you stand there with a big grin on your face.

TAPE
GLASS
TO
TABLE

The Tissue Tease

Craftily turn three pieces of wadded-up tissue paper into one piece of tissue paper with a secret message.

What You'll Need

- felt pen
- 1 large piece of tissue paper and 3 small pieces of tissue paper

Getting Ready

With the felt pen, write "Keep litter off the streets" in big letters on the large piece of tissue paper. Crumple it up into a ball and put it in your jacket pocket. Crumple up the other three pieces into balls. The audience will see these during the trick. (Instead of tissue paper you can use a heavy paper napkin. Unfold it completely. Cut off one-quarter for the big piece. Cut another quarter of it into three equal pieces to make the paper balls.)

Show Time!

1. Place the three little paper balls on the table in front of you.
2. Pick up two balls and put them in your left hand. Show the audience.
3. Pick up the third ball and put it in your pocket. Pull it out again as if you were changing your mind, but bring out the bigger tissue ball at the same time, hidden in the palm of your hand.
4. Place the third ball in your left hand with the other two. Immediately put your hands together and wad all the pieces of paper together with the big one.
5. With your left hand remove the *big piece only* from the wad now in your right hand. Make the audience think you've got nothing left in your hand by palming the three small balls and moving your fingers naturally.
6. Throw the big wad of paper into the audience as you casually place the small group into your pocket.
7. Ask the person in the audience who caught the wad to open it up. He or she will expect to find three balls. They'll be amazed to find *one* piece of paper with the very smart message!

SECRETLY EXCHANGE PAPER BALLS

SHOW OTHER TWO PAPER BALLS TO AUDIENCE

The Last Drop

By adding one more drop of water to a glass, make it impossible for a volunteer to lift the glass from a book.

What You'll Need

- hardcover book
- empty plastic tumbler
- pitcher of water
- large handkerchief
- eyedropper

Show Time!

1. Invite a volunteer onstage.
2. Hold the book in your right hand with your thumb on top of the book and your fingers below the book. Place the plastic tumbler on top of it. Pour the water from the pitcher into the tumbler until it is half full.
3. Cover the book and tumbler with the handkerchief.
4. Ask the volunteer to pick up the tumbler from the top through the handkerchief.
5. After the volunteer does this easily, ask him or her to set the tumbler down again. Remove the handkerchief and add one drop of water to the tumbler using the eyedropper.
6. Cover the book and the tumbler again with the handkerchief. Quickly shift your fingers under the handkerchief so that your thumb and pointer are above the book and holding tight to the bottom of the tumbler. The rest of your fingers are under the book. Steady the book with your other hand if you need to, but let the volunteer see that hand *above* the handkerchief. As you shift your fingers with a quick move explain that you forgot to say the magic words, "Hocus Pocus," that will make it impossible for him to pick up the tumbler this time.
7. Ask the volunteer to pick up the tumbler again. Because you are holding it by the bottom, he won't be able to move it at all!

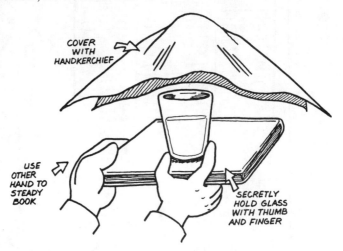

COVER WITH HANDKERCHIEF

USE OTHER HAND TO STEADY BOOK

SECRETLY HOLD GLASS WITH THUMB AND FINGER

Super Paper

Turn an ordinary sheet of newspaper comics into a bouncing ball.

What You'll Need

- hard rubber ball
- double-sided adhesive tape
- single sheet of newspaper comics

Getting Ready

Tape the ball to the top right-hand corner of the comics page in a criss-cross fashion (A).

Show Time!

1. Hold the paper in front of you by its upper corners with the ball facing you and cupped inside your right hand (B).
2. Say, "Believe it or not, I'm going to turn this funny page into a funny bouncing ball." Tightly crumple the paper around the rubber ball, and show the audience your great paper ball.
3. Chances are your audience won't be too impressed. That is, until you bounce it, and it comes right back up to your hand!

Ⓐ SECRETLY TAPE BALL TO TOP RIGHT HAND CORNER

Ⓑ CUP BALL INSIDE RIGHT HAND

Zap Ball

With ease and grace, you can make a rubber ball vanish into thin air!

What You'll Need

- 12 inches of black elastic cord
- small rubber ball
- tack
- pants with belt loops

Getting Ready

A useful part of any magician's tools is his or her clothing. In this trick, belt loops on pants serve as a quick spring-like device to make a rubber ball look as if it has vanished into thin air. To set up the trick, attach one end of the elastic cord to your middle belt loop (the one directly below your back). String the cord through all the loops on your left side except for any that might show when your magician's coat is not buttoned.

Next, attach the rubber ball to the other end of the cord with the tack. The elastic needs to be as long as the distance between the back belt loop and the first completely hidden belt loop. That first loop stops the ball from swinging away from you and keeps the ball within your reach, too.

Show Time!

1. As you complete the previous magic trick, take the rubber ball in your left hand and position yourself so your left side faces the audience. You want them to see the ball but not where it came from—pretend to have taken it out of your pants pocket. Because your left arm will be blocking the elastic from the audience's sight, the rubber ball will look perfectly normal.
2. With the rubber ball in front of you, the elastic will be stretched fairly tightly. Let go quickly, and no one will see the ball escape inside your jacket.

NOTE: This trick happens so quickly, it is more effective to perform it in silence. It does, however, require lots of practice to be pulled off effectively.

ATTACH ONE END OF ELASTIC TO BACK BELT LOOP; ATTACH OTHER END TO BALL

Ball Gone

With the flourish of a silk handkerchief, you can make a rubber ball disappear!

What You'll Need

- small rubber band
- multicolored silk handkerchief
- small rubber ball

Getting Ready

Find a handkerchief with as much design and color as you can. Secretly place the rubber band around the tips of your fingers on your left hand. Lay the handkerchief over your left hand, fingers pointing up (A). This won't be easy to do during a performance. You can either go off stage and come out again with the handkerchief draped across your hand, or, with practice, you can hide your hands below the tabletop so your audience can't see you put on the rubber band. Place the handkerchief over your hand as you stand up straight again.

Show Time!

1. Poke one of your right fingers down into the center of the rubber band to form a pocket in the handkerchief. The audience will not be able to see the rubber band.
2. Place the ball into the pocket (A) and close your left fist and your right fist around it and the handkerchief. Say, "This little ball will now disappear before your very eyes."
3. With your right hand, grasp one corner of the handkerchief and give it a quick shake, while letting go with your left hand. The ball will be gone!
4. After you grasp and shake the handkerchief, hold it down at your side so the audience will not notice the "secret compartment (B)."

THE SECRET: the tight rubber band will close around the ball, making a neat secret compartment!

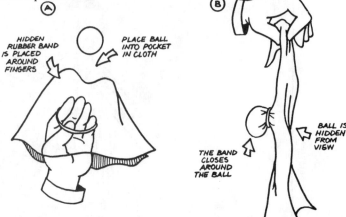

HIDDEN RUBBER BAND IS PLACED AROUND FINGERS

PLACE BALL INTO POCKET IN CLOTH

BALL IS HIDDEN FROM VIEW

THE BAND CLOSES AROUND THE BALL

The Ball Tube

A ball is dropped into a long tube. At your command, the ball stops and starts again until it finally drops through the other end.

What You'll Need

- cardboard mailing tube
- long sturdy needle
- black thread
- ball that fits snugly in the tube but rolls through easily
- small black bead
- black tempera paint
- paintbrush
- glitter
- glue
- ruler

Getting Ready

To make the tube, paint the mailing tube solid black and let it dry completely. Use the needle to poke a hole in the tube about seven inches from the end. Poke another hole directly across from the first hole. Thread the needle and push it into one hole and out the other hole. Tie a knot at the end of the thread to stop it from going all the way through.

Next, string the bead onto the thread. Tie the bead to the outside end of the thread so that when the bead is touching the tube, the thread inside the tube is loose (about twice the width of the tube) (A). When the bead is pulled away from the tube, the thread should be pulled tight across the inside of the tube.

Decorate the tube with different colors of glitter in any pattern you like.

Show Time!

1. Hold the tube straight up and down so that the bead is hidden under your thumb. With the bead in position next to the tube, drop the ball in the tube. It will fall right through.
2. Secretly pull the bead along the side of the tube with your thumb and drop the ball in the tube again. This time, the ball will seem to be magically suspended inside the tube (B). It won't fall out!
3. Secretly let go of the bead, and the ball will tumble out again!

Repeat this trick a few times for added effect.

Ⓐ THREAD RUNS THROUGH TUBE AND IS FIXED TO BEAD

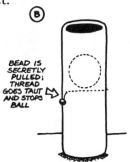

Ⓑ BEAD IS SECRETLY PULLED; THREAD GOES TAUT AND STOPS BALL

Strawberry Milk

This is a famous trick performed by many magicians including the Amazing Randi. Here are the steps and directions to make it especially easy.

In this amazing trick, the audience will see you turn plain milk into strawberry milk with only a piece of fabric!

What You'll Need

- construction paper, any color
- clear adhesive tape
- piece of white cloth
- 2 glasses
- container of milk
- red food coloring
- piece of cloth with red strawberries on it (bought at fabric store)
- stirring wand
- eyedropper

Getting Ready

Roll up a sheet of construction paper to make a tube large enough to conceal one of the glasses. Fasten it with tape. Next, make a cone with another sheet of paper. The pointed end should fit inside the other glass. Before fastening the cone with tape, make a secret pocket with a square of construction paper of the same color. Tape three sides down, leaving the fourth open. Then roll up the cone with the pocket on the inside and fasten the cone together with the tape.

Next, fold the white cloth and slide it into the secret pocket in the cone.

To prepare the table, set the cone, one empty glass, and the piece of strawberry cloth on one side of the table. On the other side, set the tube, the container of milk, and the other glass. Put 3 to 4 drops of the red food coloring into this glass. No one will see them.

Show Time!

1. Place the pointed end of the cone into the empty glass on one side of the table.
2. Stand the tube on end on the other side of the table. Put the second glass into it.

WHITE CLOTH IS HIDDEN IN CONE

TUMBLER WITH A FEW DROPS OF RED FOOD COLORING INSIDE TUBE

3. Pour the milk from the container into the glass that is in the tube.
4. Hold the strawberry cloth up to the audience for inspection. Carefully fold it up as flat as possible and slide it into the secret pocket of the cone alongside the piece of white cloth. (Practice this before the performance until you can do it smoothly without looking like you are setting anything up.)
5. With the wand, pretend to stir the cloth around in the cone. Next, stir the milk in the glass inside the tube.
6. Tell the audience that the strawberries have been magically removed from the cloth and transferred to the milk.
7. Lift the *plain* cloth out of the cone and show it to the audience.
8. Lift the tube to reveal the glass of pink milk! "Boy, I love strawberry milk," you say. Take a sip! "Mmmm."

Ribbons Around Us

Pull yards and yards of ribbon from an empty hat!

What You'll Need

- 2 to 3 tightly wound colored paper ribbon rolls
- hat with an inner band

Getting Ready

Before the magic show begins, tuck all the rolls of ribbon under the band inside the hat.

Show Time!

1. Pick up the hat from the table. Put it on and spin it around, then take it off and show the audience both the inside and the outside. The band should hold the ribbons securely.
2. After everyone is convinced the hat is empty, set it forcefully upside down on the table. The ribbon rolls should drop into the bottom of the hat.
3. Reach into the hat and grab the ends of the rolls. Hold your other hand over the top of the hat and pull the ribbons up through your fingers from your supposedly empty hat!

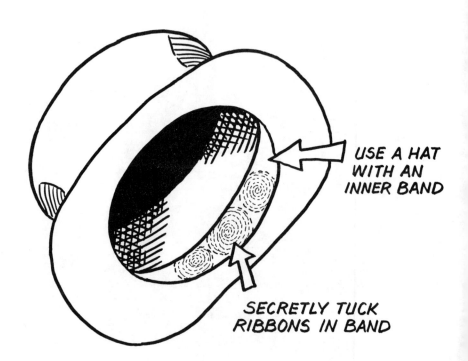

USE A HAT WITH AN INNER BAND

SECRETLY TUCK RIBBONS IN BAND

Breakthrough!

A volunteer magically escapes after being tied up!

What You'll Need

- 2 five-foot pieces of non-elastic cord or light-to-medium rope
- five-inch piece of thread
- 3 volunteers

Getting Ready

To make this trick work, both ropes are folded in half. The thread is used to tie a loop around the two folded ends. The loop is covered, and the illusion of two long, single ropes is created. In this trick, you need only a fist to cover the secret loop (A).

Show Time!

1. Have three volunteers stand side-by-side on stage, facing the audience. The two people on the end should stand forward, closer to the audience.
2. Holding the ropes with your fist clasped tightly around the secret loop in the middle, approach the volunteer in the middle.

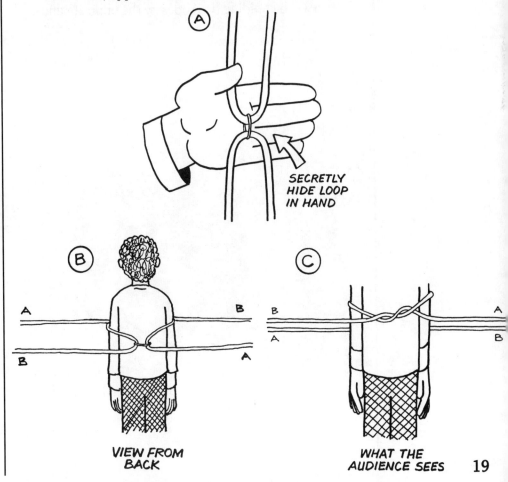

SECRETLY HIDE LOOP IN HAND

VIEW FROM BACK

WHAT THE AUDIENCE SEES

19

3. Stand in front of that volunteer with your back to the audience. Bring the ropes over the volunteer's head and place them against his or her back. The secret loop should be in the center of the volunteer's back.
4. Ask the volunteer to hold the ropes loosely with both hands at each side.
5. Give the left ends of the ropes to the volunteer on the left and the right ends to the volunteer on the right. The result should look as though the outer volunteers are holding two long ropes and the middle volunteer is standing in front of the ropes (B).
6. Take one end from each of the outer volunteers.
7. Tie the ends loosely around the front of the middle volunteer's waist.
8. Step 7 will have switched the ends of the rope. Give each switched end to the outer volunteers. The middle one now appears to be bound by the ropes (C).
9. Ask the volunteers holding the ends of the ropes to pull hard on the count of three. The middle volunteer will be free from the ropes and the other two will be holding two ropes by the opposite ends!

Lions And Tigers

A member of the audience will see lions and tigers with the mention of just two magic words!

What You'll Need

- paper
- pencil

Show Time!

1. Ask a volunteer to stand up in the audience.
2. Tell him that you know two magic words that will make him see lions and tigers. Ask him to close his eyes.
3. While the volunteer's eyes are closed, write the words "lions" and "tigers" on the piece of paper.
4. Tell him to open his eyes. Ask, "What do you see?"
5. The volunteer will have no choice but to say "lions and tigers!!"

Balloon Magic

Pop a balloon and watch it magically change colors!

What You'll Need

- light-colored balloon and dark-colored balloon (do not inflate them)
- straight pin

Getting Ready

Before your show, stuff the light-colored balloon into the dark one, making sure the mouths of the balloons stay together. Tuck the pin into the sleeve of your jacket.

Show Time!

1. Blow up the two balloons together.
2. Hold the mouth of the inner balloon closed and breathe a little more air into the outer balloon. Pinch both openings tight (A).
3. Hold the balloon up for the audience to see.
4. Casually remove the pin from your sleeve. Pass your hand over the balloon a few times. Pop the outer balloon (B). It will automatically "change" to a light color!

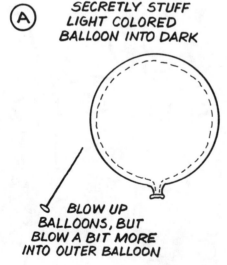

Ⓐ SECRETLY STUFF LIGHT COLORED BALLOON INTO DARK

BLOW UP BALLOONS, BUT BLOW A BIT MORE INTO OUTER BALLOON

Ⓑ POP!

USE PIN TO POP OUTER BALLOON

Flea Circus

You have trained your pet flea to perform for a live audience!

What You'll Need

- blank sheet of paper
- wooden pencil
- small box with lid

Getting Ready

Preparing for this trick requires a little bit of practice. Hold the paper in your hand with the pencil underneath it. Practice pressing the paper hard against the pencil with your thumb. Slightly moving the paper forward with your thumb will create a small *pop*. Before you go onstage, put the little box in your pocket.

Show Time!

1. Tell a story about your remarkable flea named Fleaberta. The story can be told however you like, but these are the basic elements:
   Fleaberta is an invisible flea who used to perform with gypsy fleas on pets in France. She traveled here on the back of a sailor's parrot. You found her in front of the flea market performing stunning acrobatic tricks.
2. "Fleaberta will now perform," you say. With your empty hand, reach into your pocket for the box.
3. Put the box on the table and open it. Say, "Fleaberta, would you join us, please?"
4. Pretend Fleaberta has jumped into your hand by following her with your eyes.
5. Hold Fleaberta out to your side in the palm of your hand. Hold the paper out at your other side to create a surface.
6. Toss Fleaberta into the air over your head. Follow her with your eyes until she reaches the paper. Pop the paper with the pencil when you think Fleaberta has had long enough to flip and land on the paper.
7. Ask Fleaberta to perform many stunts. Make them complex. Make them funny! It's all in how you move your eyes!
8. Make sure Fleaberta receives a nice round of applause.

Termite Damage

Another bugged trick! Discover termites in your pencil. Let everyone hear them!

What You'll Need

- wooden pencil
- paper

Show Time!

1. Take the pencil from your pocket and get ready to write on the paper.
2. Stop suddenly and hold the pencil to your ear as if you've heard something.
3. Exclaim, "Gee! I thought I had those termites exterminated!"
4. Everyone will look at you as if you're crazy, but try to convince them that there are termites in your pencil. "They *were* exterminated, but now they're back."
5. Pick a volunteer and hold the pencil up to his ear. With your hand next to his ear but away from his vision, scratch the pencil gently with your fingernail. The person *will* hear termites!

SCRATCH! SCRATCH!

Napkin Action

In this trick of wit and smarts, you can impress your audience with your strength as you pick up a whole bucket of rocks with just a paper napkin!

What You'll Need

- small bucket with handle
- enough small and medium-sized rocks to fill the bucket
- several paper napkins

Getting Ready

Test different napkins before performing this trick. Find one that is weak when open and strong when twisted up. Then, fill the bucket with rocks. Set it on the table just before you perform this trick. Unfold all the napkins and pile them up next to the bucket.

Show Time!

1. Ask your audience, "How many of these rocks in the bucket do you think you can lift 12 inches off the table with one napkin?"
2. Let a few volunteers try to do this. Most will put the rocks on a napkin and the napkin will definitely break.
3. Say, "I'll bet I can lift all the rocks in the pail with just one napkin!"
4. Lay an unfolded napkin on the table. Fold it over 3 or 4 times to make a thick strip.
5. Twist the strip. The napkin is suddenly much stronger!
6. Slide the napkin under the handle of the bucket, and lift.

Ice Slice

Cut a piece of ice in two, but see it remain in one single piece!

What You'll Need

- piece of thin, strong wire 9 to 12 inches long
- 2 pencils
- empty glass bottle, such as a soft drink or ketchup bottle
- ice cube kept in the freezer until you are ready to use it

Getting Ready

First you will need to make a tool to slice your ice cube. Take one pencil and wrap one end of the wire around the middle several times. Take the other pencil and do the same thing with the other end of the wire. The wire will cut through the ice and the pencils will serve as grips or handles.

Show Time!

1. Take the ice cube from the freezer and place it on top of the empty bottle.
2. Place the wire over the top of the ice cube so that it will slice through the middle of the cube.
3. Slowly, pull the wire down through the ice cube by firmly holding the pencil handles. It should take 3 to 7 minutes to cut through the ice. Have your assistant hold onto the bottom of the bottle to help steady it. In the meantime, you can tell a joke or you may want to build the suspense by being absolutely quiet. A drum roll is always effective!
4. Once the wire is close to cutting all the way through the ice, tell the audience that something incredible is about to happen. Keep cutting. The wire will touch the top of the glass bottle. Let the pencil handles drop and dangle from either side of the bottle. Pick up the ice cube. The audience will be amazed to see that the ice cube is still in one *uncut* piece!

NOTE: The trick is to allow enough time to let the ice *refreeze* after the wire has cut through it. Don't become impatient and cut too fast!

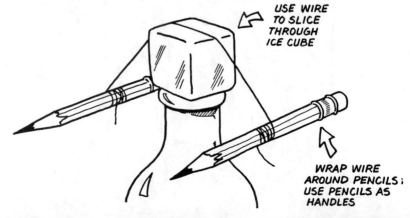

USE WIRE TO SLICE THROUGH ICE CUBE

WRAP WIRE AROUND PENCILS ; USE PENCILS AS HANDLES

Spooky Shenanigans

In this trick, spooks seem to toss a wide array of objects over a shield made by a handkerchief that you hold with *both* hands.

What You'll Need

- straight pin
- large handkerchief
- ruler
- pencil
- small bell
- deck of cards
- set of keys

Getting Ready

Attach the pin to one corner of the handkerchief. Set all the items, except the handkerchief, on the table in front of you. Place the handkerchief in a bundle next to the pile of objects.

Show Time!

1. Show the various items on the table to the audience.
2. Pick up the handkerchief. Hold the corner with the pin in your right hand and the adjacent corner with your left hand. Keep the pin hidden in your fingertips (A).

HIDDEN PIN

SECRETLY USE PIN TO AFFIX HANKY TO SLEEVE

WITH HIDDEN FREE HAND, TOSS ITEMS FROM BEHIND CLOTH

3. Holding the handkerchief as described in Step 2, revolve your arms so your right hand moves in toward your left armpit and your left hand moves out toward your right shoulder (B).
4. Lower the handkerchief's bottom edge to the table so that it conceals all the objects behind it.
5. Secretly pull the pin from the corner of the handkerchief with your right hand (this takes practice!) and attach the pin and the corner of the handkerchief to your left sleeve close to your armpit.
6. Tell the audience something really spooky is going to happen ("Now, for the *really* spooky part!").
7. Your right hand is now free to move around because the corner of the handkerchief is secretly pinned to your jacket! Toss the items from behind the cloth, over the top, toward the audience (C). They'll howl with delight!
8. To end the trick, simply remove the pin from your sleeve and revolve your arms back to their original position. The spooks are gone!!

Magic Bottle

Watch a bottle dangle from a rope too thin to hold it!

What You'll Need

- glass bottle
- small rubber ball
- 1 to 2 feet of thin cord or rope
- opaque paint
- paintbrush

Getting Ready

Paint the bottle to make it totally opaque. Find a ball that, when placed side by side with the rope, will equal the diameter of the neck of the bottle. Slip the ball into the bottle before you perform this trick.

Show Time!

1. Hold the bottle in one hand in front of the audience.
2. At the same time, hold the rope in your other hand.
3. Lower the rope into the bottle, slowly turning the bottle upside down. The ball will fall into the neck of the bottle and wedge against the rope.
4. Pull the rope out toward you just slightly. This action will tighten the wedge inside.
5. Take the free end of the rope and hold it up. The bottle magically hangs from the rope without falling!

HIDDEN BALL WEDGES ROPE IN NECK OF BOTTLE

Finger Frustration

With the mere wave of a wand, freeze an unsuspecting volunteer's fingers together! This is a great beginner's magic trick and most people love to be included in it. It is a great crowd gatherer. Try this one on your friends at school!

Show Time!

1. Ask a friend to volunteer. "It's for an experiment!" you say.
2. Tell your friend to make fists and put them together, palms down, knuckle to knuckle.
3. Ask her to extend both ring fingers upward so their tips touch. The knuckles should still be touching. This is not an easy move for most. It may take awhile.
4. Wave your hands or magic wand over your friend's hands. Say, "You now have been drained of all power from your ring fingers." (You can laugh devilishly for added effect.)
5. What you see next is hilarious. Nothing happens! It is impossible to move the two fingers apart!

NOTE: This trick is even funnier if you have several volunteers at one time—try your whole classroom!

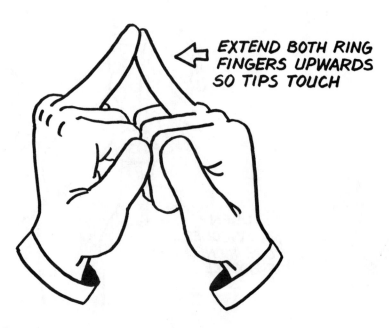

EXTEND BOTH RING FINGERS UPWARDS SO TIPS TOUCH

Mind Reader

Learn how to be a mind reader in this deceptive magic trick!

- 5 to 6 different issues of the same magazine
- 5 to 6 copies of *one* issue of the *same* magazine
- paste
- scissors

Getting Ready

Before you perform this trick, find a magazine with page numbers. Cut off the front and back covers from all the different issues. Carefully paste the different covers onto the copies of the same issue. Place the "glued" magazines on the table in a pile when you are ready to perform the trick.

Show Time!

1. Invite a volunteer to pick up any of the magazines lying on the table.
2. Ask her to look at the last page number in that particular issue. Have her choose a number between one and the last page number and tell you that number.

USE MAGAZINES WITH PAGE NUMBERS

PASTE DIFFERENT COVERS ON COPIES OF SAME ISSUE

3. Pick up another magazine from the pile as if you are going to demonstrate to the volunteer what you want her to do. Make sure she sees only the cover of your magazine so she'll think it's indeed a different issue than the one she picked.

4. Ask her to turn to the page number she selected. Remind her what it is. Say, "Please concentrate very hard as you look at that page. Hold it to your head." Demonstrate how it should be done by opening the magazine to the page that was picked and glancing over it quickly, remembering photos and headlines.

5. As your volunteer holds the magazine to her head, pretend to be able to read her mind.

6. She'll be awfully surprised when you're able to give brief details of the page that she picked!

Some Enchanted Salt Shaker

Lift a salt shaker magically into the air without using your fingertips!

What You'll Need

- toothpick
- ring for your ring finger
- salt shaker

Getting Ready

Put the ring on. Hide the toothpick by tucking the end of it under the ring on the inside of your finger. Place the salt shaker on the table.

Show Time!

1. Slowly lower your hand, palm down, over the salt shaker on the table. Insert the secret toothpick firmly into one of the holes in the cap.
2. The back of your hand will be facing the audience to conceal the toothpick. Your fingertips should point down toward the table.
3. Pretend to levitate the salt shaker with your fingertips. The toothpick will stay in the shaker hole if it is jammed in tightly. This will mesmerize your audience!

SECRETLY INSERT TOOTHPICK INTO ONE OF THE HOLES IN THE CAP

My Thumb, Please!

In this beginner's magic trick, create a real shiver when you ask someone to hold something for you.

What You'll Need

- carrot
- handkerchief

Getting Ready

Find a carrot with a tip that is about the size of your thumb. Carefully cut a length of the carrot that matches the length of your thumb, and hide it in your fist.

Show Time!

1. Cover your fist with the handkerchief.
2. Poke the carrot up so it looks like your thumb under the handkerchief.
3. Ask someone to please hold your thumb through the handkerchief.
4. Once he has a good grasp of it, simply walk away with your thumb tucked into your palm. He's left holding what he thinks is your thumb!

HOLD CARROT IN HAND

Slip Knot

This amazing trick is easy but makes you look like a genius!

What You'll Need

• 1 silky handkerchief

Getting Ready

Before the magic show begins, tie a tight knot in one corner of the handkerchief.

Show Time!

1. Hold the handkerchief by its knotted corner, hiding the knot in your thumb and fingers.
2. Point to the lower end of the handkerchief, saying that you can shake the handkerchief so hard its free corner will knot back up on itself.
3. Bring the free corner up to your fingertips and the hidden corner. Shake the free end back down again.
4. Repeat Step 3 three or four times.
5. The last time you do this, shake the handkerchief extra hard, and release the knotted end instead. This move fools everyone. The audience will be astounded.

HIDE KNOT IN HAND

Not A Knot

This amazing little knot trick will keep your friends guessing for a long time!

What You'll Need

- magic wand
- handkerchief

Getting Ready

A magic wand can easily be made from the cardboard tube that is found on most hangers that come from the dry cleaner. Paint the tube black. Make white tips at both ends with white tape or construction paper. Glue thumbtacks to the ends to give your wand "tap-ability." Sprinkle on a little glitter or give it a nice shiny coat of varnish.

Show Time!

1. Ask a volunteer to help you undo a "double-twisting-sidewinding knot."
2. Have her hold one end of the wand and point the other at you while keeping it level.

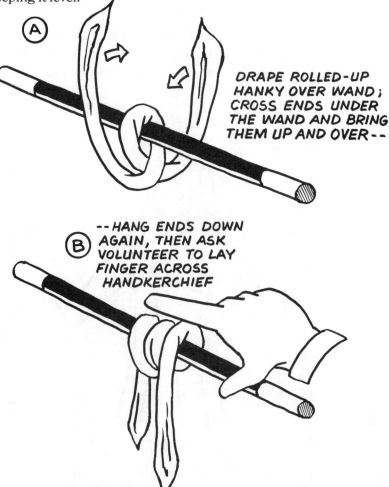

(A) DRAPE ROLLED-UP HANKY OVER WAND; CROSS ENDS UNDER THE WAND AND BRING THEM UP AND OVER--

--HANG ENDS DOWN AGAIN, THEN ASK (B) VOLUNTEER TO LAY FINGER ACROSS HANDKERCHIEF

3. Take the handkerchief by one corner and roll it up tightly.
4. Drape the rolled handkerchief over the wand so both ends hang evenly.
5. Cross the ends underneath the wand, and bring them up and over the wand, so the ends hang down again (A).
6. Ask your volunteer to please lay her finger along the wand over the handkerchief (B).
7. Repeat Step 5, but this time in the opposite direction. Bring the ends up and over your volunteer's finger, across, and down again (C), then up again so you can tie a knot over her finger (D).
8. Say, "By the time my helper moves her finger, this knot will have magically dissolved."
9. Hold the knot on top of the volunteer's finger and the loose end of your wand as well.
10. Ask her to pull her finger away quickly. Presto! No knot!

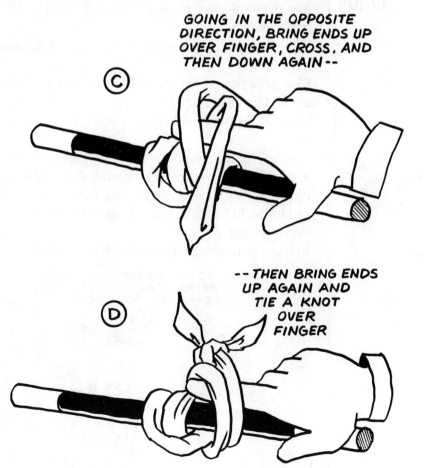

GOING IN THE OPPOSITE DIRECTION, BRING ENDS UP OVER FINGER, CROSS, AND THEN DOWN AGAIN --

©

--THEN BRING ENDS UP AGAIN AND TIE A KNOT OVER FINGER

Ⓓ

30 Presto Hanky

In this complex trick, you will make a colorful handkerchief not only jump from one location to another but reappear tied *between* two other hand-kerchiefs!

What You'll Need

- 2 single sheets of newspaper
- glue
- whole newspaper
- 2 large red handkerchiefs
- 2 identical multi-colored handkerchiefs or scarves with red borders
- empty goblet

Getting Ready

Make a secret envelope by gluing three sides of the single sheets of news-paper together. Leave a long side open (A). Place your newspaper "envelope" into the whole newspaper so it fits in normally, and keep it handy for the performance.

To prepare the handkerchief, follow these directions and look carefully at the illustrations.

First, take one corner of a red handkerchief and tie it to a corner of a multi-colored handkerchief (B). Pick them up by the knot.

Next, lay the two handkerchiefs on a table, with the multicolored hanky on top.

Now, roll up the multicolored hanky lengthwise (C). Fold the roll back over itself so only the red border protrudes beyond the knot (D).

Finally, roll up the red handkerchief around the folded part (E). The final result should look like one red hanky rolled up. There should be no trace of the other one.

Roll up the remaining red hanky. It should look like the other one. Place both on the table.

TO MAKE NEWSPAPER CONE, SECRETLY GLUE THREE SIDES; LEAVE THE LONG SIDE OPEN

(A)

GLUE

GLUE

GLUE

Show Time!

1. Hold the "magic" hanky in one hand with your thumb and forefinger around the knot. Hold the other red hanky in your other hand about one inch from the top corner. The two hankies should look exactly the same.
2. Tie the top corners of the hankies together. (The multicolored one should still be hidden inside.)
3. Wad the "two" hankies together, and stuff them into the empty goblet (F).
4. Next, you need to make a paper cone. Naturally, you reach into your handy newspaper and pull out the ordinary-looking single sheet of newspaper that you previously turned into a secret envelope.
5. Roll this sheet into a cone and hang onto it with one hand.
6. Take the remaining multicolored handkerchief, fold it in quarters neatly with your free hand, and pretend to slip it into the cone, but actually slip it into the big pocket you created.

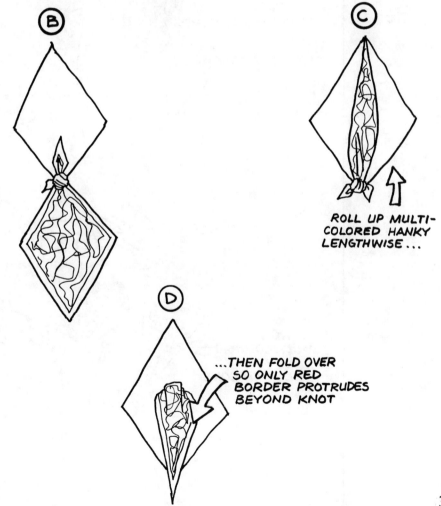

ROLL UP MULTI-
COLORED HANKY
LENGTHWISE...

...THEN FOLD OVER
SO ONLY RED
BORDER PROTRUDES
BEYOND KNOT

7. Tell the audience that with the magic word "Shazam!" you will make the hanky in the cone join the red hankies in the goblet.
8. Reach into the goblet and quickly pull out one free corner of the hankies. The multicolored one will amazingly be tied between the red hankies!
9. Unroll the newspaper cone and show both sides of it. There will be no trace of the other multicolored handkerchief!

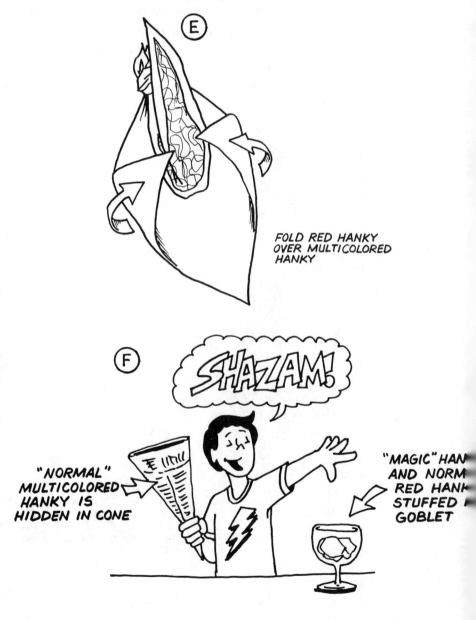

Ⓔ

FOLD RED HANKY
OVER MULTICOLORED
HANKY

Ⓕ

SHAZAM!

"NORMAL"
MULTICOLORED
HANKY IS
HIDDEN IN CONE

"MAGIC" HAN
AND NORM
RED HANK
STUFFED
GOBLET

31 The Ching-Chang Handkerchief Basket

With the mystical ching-chang basket, turn paper confetti into silk handkerchiefs!

What You'll Need

- large glass jar
- enough paper confetti to almost fill it
- black thread
- shallow basket
- 4 or 5 silky handkerchiefs

Getting Ready

Fill the glass jar ¾ full with brightly colored confetti. Tie one end of the thread to the edge of the basket. Cut the thread so that it is ¾ the diameter of the basket opening. Next, bundle up the 4 or 5 handkerchiefs and tie the other end of the thread around them. Before your performance, hide the bundle of handkerchiefs in the middle of the confetti in the jar. Set the basket right-side-up on top of the jar.

Show Time!

1. Pick up the basket in both hands and hold its open side toward the audience. The black thread will hang into the jar from the *bottom* edge of the basket. The audience will see just an empty basket with a jar of confetti underneath it (A).
2. Tip the basket forward, until its underside is facing the audience. As you do this, lower the basket so its edge just covers the top of the jar. The handkerchiefs will be pulled out of the jar and tipped into the basket without the audience seeing (B).
3. Continue to turn the basket in the same direction until it is right side up. Now hold the basket in the palm of one of your hands.
4. Reach into the jar with your free hand. Pull out some confetti and toss it in the air so it sprinkles down into the basket.
5. Pull out the handkerchiefs one by one from the supposedly empty basket! With practice this trick can be so beautifully and smoothly performed that even you will be astonished!

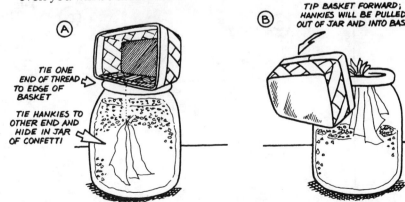

Ⓐ TIE ONE END OF THREAD TO EDGE OF BASKET

TIE HANKIES TO OTHER END AND HIDE IN JAR OF CONFETTI

Ⓑ TIP BASKET FORWARD; HANKIES WILL BE PULLED OUT OF JAR AND INTO BASKET

Out of Order

Roll up three hankies in a special order. Unroll them and they will be lined up differently!

What You'll Need

- 3 different colored handkerchiefs or cloth napkins

Show Time!

1. Place the hankies on a table, one on top of the other.
2. Roll them up together, starting with the hanky at the bottom of the stack (A).
3. Once two ends have flipped over as you roll them up, unroll the hankies (B). Their positions have magically changed (C)!
4. Roll them up again the same way, let *one* end flip over, and the positions will change again!

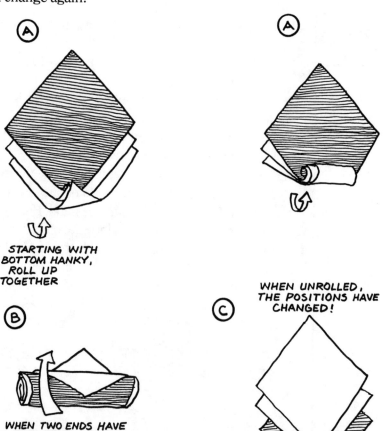

Ⓐ

STARTING WITH
BOTTOM HANKY,
ROLL UP
TOGETHER

Ⓐ

Ⓑ

WHEN TWO ENDS HAVE
FLIPPED OVER , THEN
UNROLL

Ⓒ

WHEN UNROLLED,
THE POSITIONS HAVE
CHANGED!

The Turning Box

The magical turning box is a source of great bewilderment to an unsuspecting audience. In this trick you will show your audience an empty box, both inside and out. Then, with a couple of turns, you will mysteriously pull out six handkerchiefs!

What You'll Need

- rectangular tissue box
- contact paper
- paper-towel tube
- adhesive tape
- scissors
- 6 large silky handkerchiefs

Getting Ready

To make the box, cut off the top of the tissue box. Cover it completely, both inside and out, with the contact paper (A). To assemble the device that makes this trick a success, cut the paper-towel tube down to 5¼ inches long. Cover it completely with the same contact paper. Carefully cut a square in the middle of the tube about 1 inch by 1½ inches. Seal the ends of the tube with adhesive tape. Cover the tape with contact paper and neatly trim the edges.
Next, tie the ends of the handkerchiefs together and put them into the tube one by one through the square opening (A). Put the tube inside the tissue box.

Show Time!

1. Hold the box between your hands, mouth up, and tube inside.
2. Gently set the box on the table.
3. Tilt the box toward you with your left hand without lifting the box from the table. The mouth of the box should begin to face you, while the bottom faces the audience.

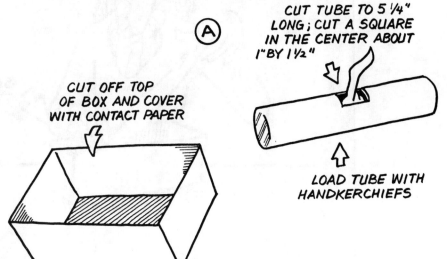

Ⓐ

CUT TUBE TO 5 ¼"
LONG; CUT A SQUARE
IN THE CENTER ABOUT
1" BY 1 ½"

CUT OFF TOP
OF BOX AND COVER
WITH CONTACT PAPER

LOAD TUBE WITH
HANDKERCHIEFS

4. Tip it a little more. The tube should roll out right in front of you. Block it with your left thumb so it doesn't roll too far. Meanwhile, tap the bottom of the box with your right hand to show that there is nothing hidden. This move draws the audience's attention away from your other hand.

5. Tip the box back to its original position. The tube is now *outside* the box, hidden behind it.

6. Tilt the box toward the audience to show its inside. The best way to do this is to slide the front bottom edge back toward yourself so you don't reveal the tube.

7. Keep turning the box in the same direction until the opening is facing you again.

8. Roll the tube back in the box with your left thumb.

9. Lift the box and place it in your right palm.

10. Reach in with your left hand, and use your fingers to hold the tube against the back side of the box.

11. Holding the box this way in your *left* hand now, reach in with your right hand and pull out the six handkerchiefs one at a time (B)!

Ⓑ

SECRETLY HOLD
TUBE IN HAND

The Disappearing Card

Here's a quick handkerchief trick to dazzle your friends!

What You'll Need

- toothpick
- handkerchief with a hem
- deck of cards
- scissors

Getting Ready

Cut the toothpick to make it the same length as the *width* of a playing card. Poke it into the hem of the handkerchief.

Show Time!

1. Spread out the deck of cards on the table.
2. Lay the handkerchief on top of the cards so that the edge with the tooth-pick in it is casually folded *underneath* the handkerchief.
3. Pick up the toothpick through the handkerchief with one hand. Hold one end between your thumb and forefinger. This will look as though you have picked up one of the cards!
4. Toss the handkerchief into the air and say, "Presto!" The card completely vanishes!

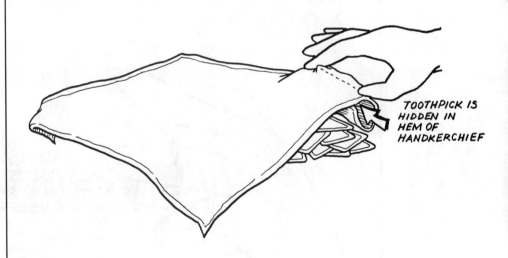

TOOTHPICK IS HIDDEN IN HEM OF HANDKERCHIEF

Good News!

Spread some fun and good news with this sneaky newspaper trick!

What You'll Need

- empty sliding drawer box (matchbox style)
- rubber band
- 4 small silky handkerchiefs (red, yellow, green, blue)
- single sheet of newspaper
- scissors

Getting Ready

First, cut one end off the drawer part of the box. Slide the cover back into place. Stuff the 4 handkerchiefs into the box through its new opening. Now, place the rubber band around the width of the box. To prepare the newspaper for this trick, cut 4 slits in the sheet in different places. They should be just big enough for a handkerchief to be pulled through them.

Before you perform the trick, place the box under the newspaper on a table.

Show Time!

1. Begin by talking about the news. Using your left arm to gesture with and draw the audience's attention, slide your right hand under the newspaper, palm down, on top of the box.
2. While you continue talking about the news, slide the middle fingers of your right hand between the rubber band and the box. The opening of the box should point toward your fingertips (A).

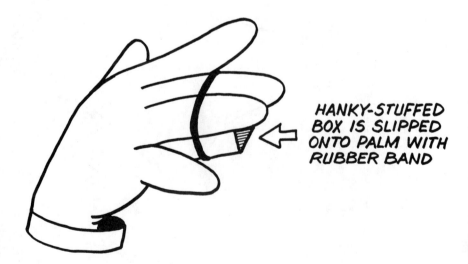

HANKY-STUFFED BOX IS SLIPPED ONTO PALM WITH RUBBER BAND

3. Sliding your right hand out from under the newspaper, grasp the paper between your thumb and fingers. If you hold the paper near the top in this manner out to your right side, no one will have seen the box attached to your palm or the rubber band (B).

4. With your left hand, point to different stories on the newspaper page. Trace your finger along the cuts in the paper as if you were reading. (Do indeed read from the paper but add your own last line to each story. You can use these endings or make up your own.)

5. As you get to your new ending of each story, reach into the cut on the paper and pull out a handkerchief! Remember in what order you put them in the box so you will know the order in which they will come out.

The endings: "So it turns out that everything ended up *rosy*!" (Pull out red handkerchief.)

"And they were *green* with envy!" (Pull out green handkerchief.)

"That car was a total *lemon*!" (Pull out the yellow handkerchief.)

"The Bobcats keep losing. They must really have the *blues*!" (Pull out the blue handkerchief.)

BOX IS "PALMED" AND HIDDEN BEHIND SLITTED PAPER

Break Out!

Just like Houdini, but on a smaller scale, remove an object from a maximum-security handkerchief! This trick even stuns volunteers from the audience.

What You'll Need

- man's large handkerchief
- large piece of black cloth
- key ring, 1 inch in diameter
- small object borrowed from the audience or supplied by you

Show Time!

1. Show the audience both sides of the open handkerchief.
2. Tell them you will trap an object in this handkerchief and then attempt to remove it by mystical means.
3. Lay the handkerchief on the table. Ask someone in the audience for a ring, a key, or a dime.
4. Place the object in the center of the open handkerchief. Draw together the far corners around it.
5. Put the key ring over the top of the corners, forming a little "prison" for the object.
6. Invite four members of the audience to help you "secure" the prison.
7. Each volunteer should take hold of one corner of the handkerchief and hold onto it tightly.
8. Drape the large black cloth over the handkerchief prison and the volunteers' hands.
9. The magic moment: simply reach under the black cloth and into the opening between the folds of the handkerchief to remove the object.
10. Show the object to the audience and the surprised volunteers. Gasps of delight will be heard!
11. Remove the black cloth from the handkerchief—the prison will be found totally intact!

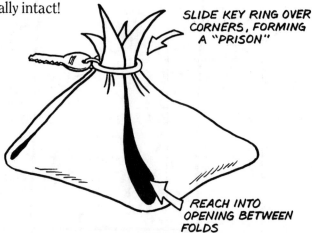

SLIDE KEY RING OVER CORNERS, FORMING A "PRISON"

REACH INTO OPENING BETWEEN FOLDS

Eggsibit

Put an egg in a hat and make it disappear!

- needle
- thread
- handkerchief
- adhesive tape

- empty eggshell (you can find these at major shops, or maybe Mom or Dad knows how to "blow out" the contents of an egg)

Getting Ready

Using the needle, tie one end of the thread to the edge of the handkerchief, right in between two corners. Attach the other end of the thread to the egg with the tape. The egg should hang almost ⅔ of the way down the handkerchief (A).

Set the hat upside down on the table. Crumple up the handkerchief around the egg to hide it, and place it next to the hat.

Show Time!

1. Show the audience the empty hat, inside and out.
2. Lift the handkerchief by its corners so that the attached egg is on *your* side of the handkerchief.

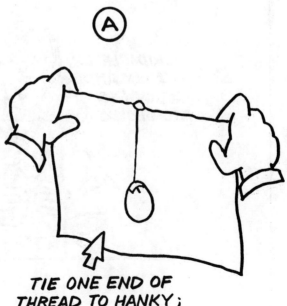

Ⓐ

TIE ONE END OF THREAD TO HANKY; ATTACH OTHER END TO EGG WITH TAPE

3. Crumple up the handkerchief again and then draw the egg up from its folds (B). Show the audience that the egg has magically appeared!
4. Next, gently place the egg in the hat with the handkerchief around it.
5. Remove the handkerchief from the hat, again holding its upper corners with the egg facing you. No one will know the egg is there.
6. Repeat steps 3, 4, and 5 two more times.
7. Say, "I'm sure you think there were three eggs hidden in here," pointing to the hat.
8. Since you've been placing each egg that "magically" appeared into the hat, surely everyone thinks that's where they are. You now say, "Well they are . . . *not!*" Turn the hat over as you say this. Of course, there will be no eggs in it!
9. You can plan a surprise ending for this trick. Look all over for the eggs. Lift up the handkerchief to look under it, and "accidentally" (but really on purpose) show the audience the string and the egg. Say "Gotcha!" Your audience will appreciate being let in on *one* trick.

Ⓑ

CRUMPLE UP
HANKY AND
DRAW EGG
FROM FOLDS

Tricky Pockets

You can create magic easily with several different day-to-day items including clothing! Here is a trick that utilizes your pants pockets.

What You'll Need

- a very large silky handkerchief
- a pair of your pants with front pockets

Getting Ready

All you have to do to get ready is examine your front pants pockets. Most pants have deep pockets, but they also have a rather large space of fabric in the upper corner that goes all the way to the zipper or buttons. What a super place to hide things! Wad or fold up the handkerchief and stuff it into this extra space before you perform this trick.

Show Time!

1. Say to the audience, "I have nothing in my hands. I have nothing in my pockets."
2. And then to prove it, turn your pockets inside out. (You can only pull out the deep part.)
3. Stuff your pockets back inside your pants.
4. Say, "I can pull a handkerchief from my pocket just by snapping my fingers."
5. Reach into your pockets again and pull out the hidden handkerchief.

NOTE: As you grasp the handkerchief, reach way down to the bottom of your pocket, so it looks as if the handkerchief came from the *bottom*, not the top, of your pocket.

PRESTO!

HANKY IS PULLED FROM TOP OF POCKET

39 The Dancing Handkerchief

A handkerchief with a mind of its own? With magic, anything can happen! Learn how to make a knotted handkerchief dance itself undone in this impressive trick.

What You'll Need

- large silky handkerchief
- needle

- 2 to 3 feet of black thread or ultra-fine clear fishing line

Getting Ready

To prepare the handkerchief, secure the thread or line to one corner of the handkerchief with the needle. Tie a good, strong knot and lay the thread back across the handkerchief.

Show Time!

1. Gather up the handkerchief and tie a single knot in the middle of it, making sure the thread or line runs right through its center.
2. Hold the *un*threaded corner of the handkerchief in your fingertips. The threaded corner should be pointed toward the floor. The thread should hang down to the floor.
3. Step on the dangling thread. Point to the handkerchief and talk about its magical qualities while you step on the thread. Say, "This handkerchief is not just a dancer, it's a fancy dancer. It can untangle itself." This is called "drawing attention."
4. Next, gently move your hand up and down, back and forth to music as if the hanky were dancing and, right before everyone's eyes, the knot will come undone all by itself!

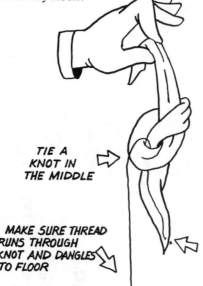

TIE A KNOT IN THE MIDDLE ⇨

MAKE SURE THREAD RUNS THROUGH KNOT AND DANGLES TO FLOOR

SECURE THREAD TO ONE CORNER

The Mystical Coin

You, the magician, can swiftly pass a mystical coin through an ordinary handkerchief!

What You'll Need

- large coin (no smaller than a quarter)
- handkerchief

Getting Ready

To get ready for this trick, you must practice. Only smooth, quick moves will give you the results you will need to astonish your audience.

Show Time!

1. Hold the coin up between your left thumb and forefinger in front of the audience.
2. Cover your left hand with the handkerchief (A).
3. Grasp the coin through the handkerchief with your right hand.
4. Fold the coin and the handkerchief toward yourself once.
5. Reach under the handkerchief, grasp the coin, and make a fold with your left hand (B).
6. Fold back the corner of the handkerchief, facing the audience, to show them the coin is still there (C).

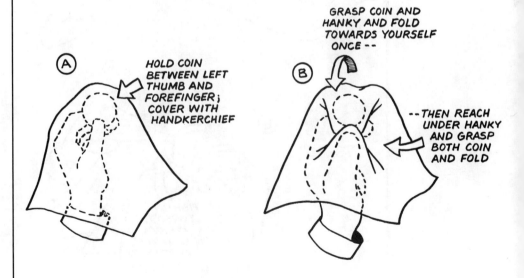

HOLD COIN BETWEEN LEFT THUMB AND FOREFINGER; COVER WITH HANDKERCHIEF

GRASP COIN AND HANKY AND FOLD TOWARDS YOURSELF ONCE --

--THEN REACH UNDER HANKY AND GRASP BOTH COIN AND FOLD

7. What makes this trick work? Cover the exposed coin again—but instead of bringing back only the one flap of handkerchief, bring over the opposite flap as well (D). To the audience, it will look as if you just covered it up again normally.
8. Tightly twist the handkerchief just under the coin. It will appear to be wrapped snugly.
9. Work the coin out of the secret opening created by the folds of hand-kerchief (E). If done smoothly, even you will think the coin has risen up through the handkerchief!

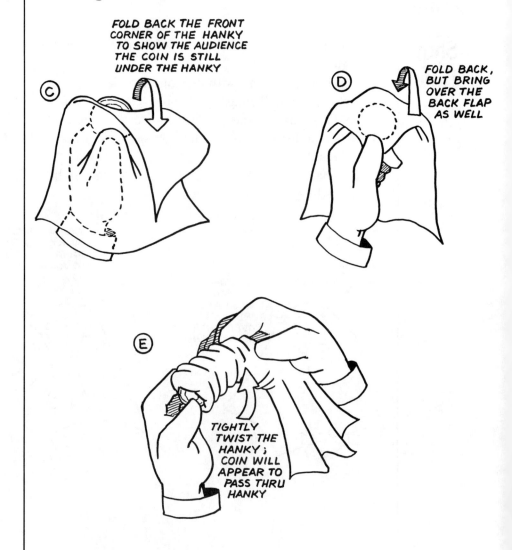

FOLD BACK THE FRONT CORNER OF THE HANKY TO SHOW THE AUDIENCE THE COIN IS STILL UNDER THE HANKY

C

D FOLD BACK, BUT BRING OVER THE BACK FLAP AS WELL

E

TIGHTLY TWIST THE HANKY; COIN WILL APPEAR TO PASS THRU HANKY

The Sound of Silver

Half the fun of magic is knowing more than your friends do, or even pretending to know more, especially strange, unusual things like the difference between the sound of copper and silver!

What You'll Need

- 2 pennies
- 1 dime
- ¼-inch strand of your hair
- clear-drying glue
- sharp pencil
- 3 twist-on bottle caps

Getting Ready

Carefully glue the strand of hair to the penny so that the tiniest bit sticks out over the edge of it, just enough to stick out from under the edge of a bottle cap placed over the penny.

Just before your show, remember to put two pennies (one special, one ordinary) and 1 dime in one of your pockets.

Show Time!

1. Reach into your pocket and pull out the change. Take the special penny and the dime and put them on the table. Ask the audience if anyone can spare another dime.
2. As soon as you are given the dime, put the three bottle tops on the table. Invite three volunteers onstage.
3. Explain that your fine-tuned ears can detect the sound of silver. To prove it, you would like them to arrange the coins underneath the bottle tops any way they wish, one coin per top. Turn your back while they do it.
4. When you turn around again, ask the audience for complete silence. Tap each top with your pencil point.
5. Since the penny has the hair attached, you know which tops have dimes under them, making it much easier to detect the silver!

GLUE HAIR
TO PENNY

Colorized

The next trick is so much fun to do—and is so unbelievable—that you will probably practice it more than any of the others just to see the ever-amazing results.

What You'll Need

• deck of cards

Getting Ready

First, arrange the deck so that the top two cards are the same number or face but are in different color suits: one 4 of diamonds and one 4 of spades, for example. After that, you just need to practice to get the trick right.

Show Time!

1. Hold the deck face down in one hand.
2. Flip up the first card.
3. Slide that card, and the one right under it, about ¾ of an inch over the side of the deck (over the left side if the deck is in your right hand, over the right side of the deck if it is in your left hand). Be sure to slide them over at the same time so they look like one (A).
4. Hold the deck in your hand, overhanded. Throw the pack firmly but neatly so the stack remains intact, onto the floor. (Be sure not to do it *too* hard or you will be picking up a lot of cards!)
5. The rush of air will flip the top cards over, making the secret second card suddenly appear on top of the stack (B)!

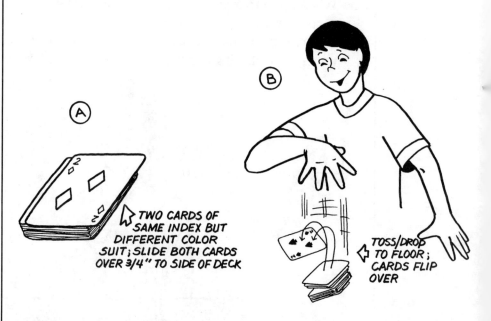

Ⓐ TWO CARDS OF SAME INDEX BUT DIFFERENT COLOR SUIT; SLIDE BOTH CARDS OVER 3/4" TO SIDE OF DECK

Ⓑ TOSS/DROP TO FLOOR; CARDS FLIP OVER

Penny-tration

Make a penny penetrate a human hand!

What You'll Need

* 7 pennies

Show Time!

1. Show your audience that you have seven pennies. Have a volunteer drop them one by one into your cupped hand and count them out loud.
2. Tell the volunteer that you can make one of the pennies pass through his hand.
3. Hold six of the pennies in your right hand and the seventh in your left. Making sure that the volunteer's hand is cupped, place the pennies into it one by one, counting them out loud. The first one won't make a noise, but the rest will clink.
4. Before you start putting the pennies in his hand, warn the volunteer that he must quickly close it once the seventh penny is dropped in.
5. When you get to the sixth penny, just clink it against the others in the volunteer's hand, and bring it out again hidden between your fingers. The seventh penny should be quickly dropped into your other hand.
6. Carefully and firmly cup your hand with the penny in it underneath the volunteer's fist so that his knuckles are facing downward.
7. Explain that it takes extreme concentration and incredible magic power to make pennies pass through skin and bones while you slowly flatten your hand against his knuckles. Now say, "Did you feel that? Look! I hold a penny in my hand. Quick! Count the pennies in your hand." Won't everyone be shocked to see only six pennies in the volunteer's hand!

PENNY IS HIDDEN IN YOUR PALM

A Head for Numbers

Use your mental powers to guess the name of a card right through a closed card box.

What You'll Need

- deck of cards
- the box in which it came
- scissors

Getting Ready

Before the start of the show, cut a very small hole in one lower corner of the box (A).

Show Time!

1. Spread the cards out on the table.
2. Hold the empty card box behind your back with its top open and facing away from you. The special hole will be facing upward. Hold it at its lower end, and cover the hole with your thumbs (B).
3. Invite anyone from the audience to pick a card from the deck, look at the card, and remember it. Then have the volunteer insert the card face up in the box and close the box while it is still in your hands behind your back.
4. The volunteer may be seated. Bring the box to your forehead. Say, "I can find out what card you had by reading your mind." As you lift the box over your eyes, glance into the hole to find out the identity of the card.
5. Place the closed box against your forehead with your eyes closed. Pretend to concentrate hard! You can even hum for effect.
6. Name the card. Your audience will be very impressed!

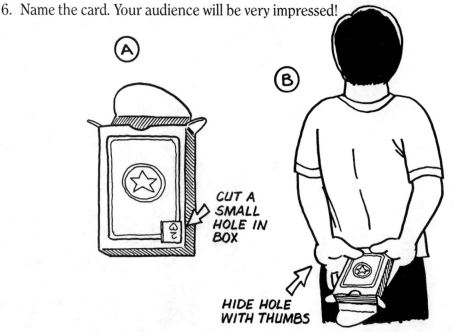

Mental Telepathy

What You'll Need

- deck of cards

Getting Ready

Before you begin, pick out any two cards from the deck and put them in your pocket.

Show Time!

1. Ask a volunteer to choose three cards and show them to you and the audience. They can be from anywhere in the deck. Ask another member of the audience to concentrate hard on one of the three cards.
2. Put the three cards in your pocket with the other two secret cards. (REMEMBER! Note the order in which you place the three cards into your pocket.)
3. Draw out the two cards that you put in your pocket before the show. Don't show them to the audience. They will appear to be two of the three you placed in your pocket a moment ago.
4. Lay the two cards face down on top of the deck.
5. Say to the second volunteer, "If you have been thinking of your card, it will be the one still in my pocket." Ask her to name the card.
6. The volunteer gives the name of one of the three cards shown earlier. Since you carefully noted the cards and their order in your pocket, simply pull the audience member's chosen card from your pocket!

Houdini's Just Passing Through

Is it possible for a person to physically pass right through a playing card? With this funny trick, it is!

What You'll Need

- playing card
- sharp pair of scissors

Getting Ready

Preparation of the playing card is everything in this trick. Since you need to cut the card several times with a pair of scissors, you may want to practice a lot. You may also want a parent or someone good with scissors to help prepare the card for you. It is also a good idea to practice with ordinary paper, then practice on jokers or cards in an incomplete deck. Steps 2–5 can be done before the magic show.

Show Time!

1. Show the audience that you have an ordinary playing card. Tell them you are going to walk through this card.
2. Fold the card lengthwise, making a sharp crease with your fingernail or a pencil.
3. Starting at one end, cut from the fold almost to the edge of the card several times. Cuts should be ⅛ inch apart (A).
4. Now make cuts from the edge, almost to the fold, in between the cuts you just made (B).
5. Cut each fold along the crease except for the outer two (C). If everything is done correctly, you will have created one very long, delicate chain, big enough for a person to pass through.
6. Ask a volunteer to hold the long chain in an arch. When you walk through the special card, everyone will be surprised!

NOTE: Once you have mastered cutting the card, you can do it right on stage!

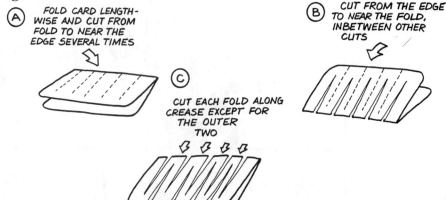

(A) FOLD CARD LENGTH-WISE AND CUT FROM FOLD TO NEAR THE EDGE SEVERAL TIMES

(B) CUT FROM THE EDGE TO NEAR THE FOLD, INBETWEEN OTHER CUTS

(C) CUT EACH FOLD ALONG CREASE EXCEPT FOR THE OUTER TWO

You can stump your friends over and over with this clever card trick.

What You'll Need

- deck of cards

Show Time!

1. Invite a member of the audience to the table to be your subject. Ask your volunteer to lay out two rows of cards, any number of them, as long as the bottom row has as many cards as the top row. You should be blindfolded or have your back to your subject. (You can even do this trick on the telephone with your subject!)
2. Instruct the volunteer to take one card away from the bottom row.
3. Now ask your volunteer to decide how many cards she would like to take from the top row. She should tell you this number and take away exactly that many cards from the top row only.
4. Now instruct her to take away from the bottom row the number of cards left in the top row.
5. Now tell the volunteer to get rid of the rest of the cards in the top row.
6. The object of having your back to the subject or being blindfolded or even on the phone is to correctly guess how many cards are left. The answer is always right if you remember the number of cards that your subject removed previously from the top row. It is always exactly *one* less than the number given!

Four Aces

Watch four aces magically jump from the pack to the table! This trick takes practice and careful, swift hand movements.

What You'll Need

- 2 decks of cards (both with the same back pattern)
- large pair of scissors
- ruler

Getting Ready

From one deck of cards, pull the ace of diamonds, ace of clubs, and ace of spades. Set the pack aside because it won't be needed anymore. Measure and cut 1/16 inch off from the bottom of each of the aces (A). Before the performance, take the three cut aces and the normal ace of hearts from the other deck of cards and set all four cards in a pile on the table. Place the remaining three normal aces seventh, eighth, and ninth from the top in the deck (B).

Show Time!

1. Tell the audience you have removed the aces from the deck. Point to the pile on the table.
2. Lay each ace face down on the table in this order: ace of clubs, ace of spades, ace of hearts, ace of diamonds. Let the audience see each one as you set it down.
3. Deal three cards from the top of the main deck on top of the ace of clubs, then the ace of spades, the ace of hearts, and finally the ace of diamonds.
4. Ask an audience member to call out 1, 2, 3, or 4. Count off each pile of cards so that no matter which number is picked, the pile with the ace of hearts is always the stack on which the count ends.
5. Put the other three piles back on the main deck. Shuffle the deck.
6. Snap the back of the deck with your finger and say "Ready." Slowly and carefully flip through the deck so the audience can see the top of each card. Surprisingly, there are no aces! (The cut aces won't be seen because they are shorter.)
7. Invite someone from the audience to turn over the stack of cards left on the table. What will be found? Four aces!

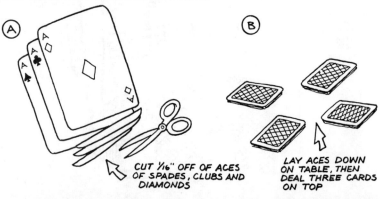

CUT 1/16" OFF OF ACES
OF SPADES, CLUBS AND
DIAMONDS

LAY ACES DOWN
ON TABLE, THEN
DEAL THREE CARDS
ON TOP

All in the Voice

A volunteer's vocal vibrations will help identify a specific card in this mind-boggling magic trick!

What You'll Need

- deck of cards

Getting Ready

Before the magic show, place the four eights at the top of the pack and the four twos at the bottom of the pack.

Show Time!

1. Have a volunteer take the deck of cards in her hand and deal out all the cards into four piles.
2. After dealing the cards, ask the volunteer to pick one card from the middle of the pile, look at it, remember it, and put it on top of another pile.
3. Ask her to stack the four piles on top of each other. Then have her flip over and name each card, one at a time. Tell your volunteer that vibrations in her voice will give away the identity of the card.
4. As each card is named, listen for the number 8. If it is followed directly by a 2, you know that the chosen card is not near. However, when the number 8 is followed by another number or face card, and then a 2, the number in between the 8 and the 2 is the chosen card!
5. Ask your volunteer to go back and name the last few again. You can then announce, "That's it! I can feel the vibrations!"

PLACE FOUR EIGHTS AT THE TOP OF THE DECK

HAVE VOLUNTEER DEAL OUT ALL THE CARDS INTO FOUR PILES

PLACE FOUR TWOS AT THE BOTTOM

Fifteen Cents

Test your friends' math wit with this brain teaser at school or at a magic show!

What You'll Need

- 1 dime
- 1 nickel

Getting Ready

Before you begin, secretly place the dime and nickel in your hand. Make a fist around the coins.

Show Time!

1. "I am holding two American coins in my hand that add up to fifteen cents. One of them is not a dime," you say.
2. Pick a volunteer to figure out the problem. The answers given will be very surprising. You may not get any answers at all!
3. When you think the volunteer has had enough, open your hand and say, "I said one of them was not a dime, and I'm right—it's a nickel!"

NOTE: Get ready to run!